WARNING

This book contains sexually explicit scenes and adult language. It may be considered offensive to some readers. This book is for sale to adults ONLY.

* * * * * * * * * * * * * * * * * * *

Please store your files wisely where they cannot be accessed by underage readers.

Please feel free to send me an email. Just know that these emails are filtered by my publisher. Good news is always welcome.

Just Plain Bob - **justplainbob@awesomeauthors.org**

About the Publisher
4Fun Publishing, a member of **BLVNP Incorporated**, 340 S. Lemon #6200, Walnut CA 91789, info@blvnp.com / legal@blvnp.com
NOTE: Due to the highly emotional reaction of some people to works of erotic fiction, any email sent to the above address that contains foul language or religious references is automatically deleted by our anti-spam software and will not be seen. All other communications are welcome.

DISCLAIMER
Please don't be stupid and kill yourself. This book is a work of FICTION. Do not try any new sexual practice that you find in this book. It is fiction and not to be confused with reality. Neither the author nor the publisher or its associates assume any responsibility for any loss, injury, death or legal consequences resulting from acting on the contents in this book. Every character in this book is over 18 years of age. The author's opinions are not to be construed as the opinions of the publisher. The material in this book is for entertainment purposes ONLY. Enjoy

JUST PLAIN BOB

Halloween
&
DRUGS

A LANDING STRIP STORY

Halloween & Drugs

A Landing Strip Story

Taboo Erotica

By: Just Plain Bob

© **Just Plain Bob 2014**
ISBN: 978-1-68030-076-5

I really didn't know why I was there. I didn't feel like drinking, but I needed to get out and do something. Sitting around the house and whining about how life had treated me wasn't getting me anywhere. I used to enjoy open microphone night at the Landing Strip and maybe a few laughs would help.

I looked around as I came in and I saw that there were some people there that I knew. I saw Angie Springer sitting at a table with three other girls. Wally Taylor and his wife Julie were there, which was a surprise. The last time I had been in the Strip on open mike night he had publicly accused Julie of being a cheating whore. Seeing them together caused me to frown. The last thing I wanted to think about on that night was cheating whores.

Up on the platform that served as a stage on mike night and a bandstand on Thursday, Friday and Saturday, Bobby Denton was telling another one of his blond jokes.

"Recently, when I went to McDonald's I saw on the menu that you could have an order of 6, 9 or 12 Chicken McNuggets. I told the teenaged blond behind the counter that I wanted a half dozen Chicken McNuggets and she looked at me and said,

"We don't have half dozen nuggets."

"You don't?" I replied.

"We only have six, nine or twelve," the blond said.

"So I can't order a half dozen, but I can get six?"

"That's right," the young blond girl said.

"So I shook my head and ordered six McNuggets."

His wife Bree was sitting in the back with some friends and fuming.

Everyone knew that Bree hated blond jokes, but Bobby didn't seem to give a shit if she liked them or not. He turned the mike over to the next hopeful and went over and sat down at the bar and talked to Melody the barmaid. I wondered why Bobby never went back and sat with his wife at her table.

Shari brought me my PBR and I sat, sipped and listened and my mood lightened. There was some pretty good talent there that night. There was a time once when I'd had a few too many in me and I was dared to get up and take a shot at it. I still remembered the joke I told that night.

"A man was sick and tired of going to work everyday while his wife stayed home. He wanted her to see what he went through so he prayed:

"Dear Lord, I go to work everyday and put in eight long hours while my wife stays at home. I want her to know what I go through so please allow her body to switch with mine for a day."

The Lord, in his infinite wisdom, granted the man his wish. The next morning, sure enough, the man awoke as a woman. He arose, cooked breakfast for his mate, awakened the kids, set out their school clothes, fed them breakfast, packed their lunches and then drove them to school. On the way home he dropped off some clothes at the cleaners and stopped by the bank to make a deposit.

He went grocery shopping and then went home and put away the groceries, sat down and paid the bills and then balanced the checkbook. He cleaned the cat's litter box and then gave the dog a bath.

By then it was 1 P.M. and he hurried to make the beds, do the laundry, vacuum, dust, sweep and mop the floors. Ran to school and picked up the kids and got into an argument with them on the way home, set out milk and cookies for them and got them organized to do their homework.

He set up the ironing board and ironed clothes while watching some TV and at 4:30 he began peeling potatoes and washing vegetables, breaded the pork chops and got dinner on the stove. After dinner, he cleaned the kitchen, ran the dishwasher, folded laundry and bathed the kids and put them to bed. At 9 P.M. he was exhausted and he went to bed where he was expected to make love which he managed to get through without complaint.

The next morning he awoke and immediately got down on his knees beside the bed.

"Lord, I don't know what I was thinking. I was so wrong to envy my wife's being able to stay home all day. Please, Oh Please let us trade back. Amen."

The Lord, in his infinite wisdom replied:

"My son, I feel that you have learned your lesson and I will be happy to change things back to the way they were. But you will have to wait nine months before I can do it. You got pregnant last night."

I was booed off the stage. I never had the nerve to try it again.

I was applauding the accountant who had just finished his stand-up routine when Angie Springer sat down at my table.

"Hi stranger," she said, "Buy a girl a drink?"

I looked over at the table where she had been sitting when I came in and saw that it was empty. She saw me look and said:

"They all had to get home to their husbands."

I raised an eyebrow at that and Angie noticed and read the unsaid "But you aren't in a hurry to get home to yours?" that the look implied.

"Gary is out of town and the kids are spending the week with my parents. I don't need to hurry home."

I waved Shari over and Angie asked for a Tom Collins and Shari went to the bar to get it.

"So how have you been?" Angie asked.

"So so…yourself?"

"About as well as can be expected. I've been wanting to talk to you for a while now, but have never had the chance."

"Talk to me? About what?"

"I want to know why you let Gary slide."

"What?"

"Please don't play stupid with me Rob. I'm not some empty headed clueless broad. I know what happened and I want to know why you let Gary slide when you burned all those other assholes."

I looked at Angie and it all came flooding back to me.

~*** ~

It started with a raffle at the Fraternal Order of Eagles. I had purchased five tickets with the expectation of not winning anything. I never had and I never expected to. The prizes for the raffle were all donated and the money from the ticket sales went to various charities that the Aerie supported so I always bought a few. The night of the drawing one of my numbers was called and I became the owner of a new state of the art security system.

I really didn't want it or need it and I tried swapping it for some of the stuff the other winners won. I was trying to convince Toby Martin that he would get more out of the security system than he would get out of a two week cruise when he told me that I wasn't looking at it in the right way.

"You know how much you like watching the porn tapes at our poker games. Use the system to make your own."

"What do you mean?"

"Put the system in and don't tell Beth about it. After you've made love a couple of times tell her that you are having sex with a porn star. She will probably come unglued on you and then you can laugh at her and show her the tapes of the two of you going at it. Also there is the monetary part."

"Monetary part?"

"Call your insurance man and tell him you have installed a security system. Most insurance companies will give you a reduced rate if you have one."

The idea appealed to me and I decided to keep the system. I made an appointment to get the system installed and then took a day off work so I could be there and watch the installation and get trained on its use.

The system came with two outside cameras and five inside cameras along with motion detectors and some other bells and whistles and the first six months of service were free, the second six were half off and then I would have to sign a yearly contract. The technician installed the outside cameras – one to cover the front of the house and one to cover the back – and then he asked me where I wanted the inside ones.

He suggested the living room because anyone who broke in would go for where the TV, DVD player and other expensive items were and that was usually the living room. Also the intruder would have to pass through the living room to get to the stairway that led upstairs. He also suggested that one be put in the basement in case the intruder gained access by breaking out a basement window.

All good ideas and I took them, but I wanted one in the bedroom and I didn't want him to know the real reason why so I told him I had a safe in the bedroom closet and I wanted a camera in the master bedroom. We had two more bedrooms and I had turned one of them into a sort of home office/den and we put the fourth one in there. The last camera went into the kitchen for no other reason than I couldn't think of where else to put it.

I had him put the keypad in the front vestibule closet and then he showed me how to operate the system. There was a recorder in one of my workshop cabinets in the basement that captured the cameras output and most important, to me anyway, was that the camera's output didn't go to the security company. No one from the company would ever see what was on the recorder unless there was a break in and then they along with the police would want to see what the cameras captured.

That night I gave the system a trial run. After dinner and an hour or so of TV I started making out with Beth on the living room couch and that led to us heading for the bedroom where we made mad passionate love. The next day while Beth was making dinner, I went down into the basement and checked the recorder. It had captured our session perfectly.

~~***~~

Over the next two weeks I made love to Beth eight times and then one Saturday while she was out grocery shopping, I pulled the DVD out of the recorder and put it in a safe place and inserted a fresh DVD into the machine. I began making plans for the night - I was going to let Beth see herself as a porn star.

I decided that I would do it on Halloween. We were going to have a party that night and when everyone left at the end of the party, I would pour Beth a glass of her favorite wine and we would watch the DVD. Her costume was going to be a very sexy Cat Woman outfit with stiletto heels and I was going to love peeling it off of her as she watched herself perform.

Three days before Halloween, I had to take a sudden overnight trip to call on a client who was having trouble with one of the machines we had sold him. I was able to correct the problem and then headed on home. I went straight home from the airport since I didn't see any sense in going in to work for only forty-five minutes and since my commute home from work was almost forty minutes, I was going to get home a good hour and a half before I was expected. As a result, I got home before Beth.

Since Beth wasn't home yet I decided that I had time to check the recorder and see if it had captured our last love making session which had been the night before I left on my trip. The recorder had captured the last love making session perfectly. There was only one problem.

The last love making session captured was of Beth and our next door neighbor Jim Case.

I say that the last session was captured, but it was a little more than that. Beth sucked him off as he sat on our living room couch and then she led him upstairs and fucked him on our bed. After cumming in Beth and pulling out he said:

"You need to get me up again lover. There is still one place in this house that I haven't marked as my territory."

"Where is that," my loving wife asked.

"His den. I want to take you on his desk."

Beth laughed and said, "You are evil," and Jim said, "And you love it."

"I love your cock too," Beth said and then went down on him. She got him back up and when he was hard they went into the den and Jim fucked her in the ass as she laid on her back on my desk with her legs up on Jim's shoulders.

"I don't think I'll ever get enough of this ass," Jim said and Beth moaned and said, "I never get tired of giving it to you."

That really ground on me because Beth wouldn't give me her ass. We had tried anal sex a couple of times, but she said it hurt too much and she didn't really like doing it.

When they finished, they went downstairs and had a drink at the kitchen table. Jim said:

"Hal wants to know when he can get together with either you or the both of us again."

"Were you able to get the stuff?"

"I pick it up tomorrow."

"Okay then, tell Hal it will be at the Halloween party on Saturday. I'll put the stuff in Rob's drink and that will knock him out. Once he is in bed and out of the way, we can party."

"You need to be careful there. If you give it all to him at once he might conk out quickly and then wonder about it. Put a little bit in each drink you give him and it will seem to him that he drank too much and got drunk. Any chance I can get another taste before the party?"

"Maybe. How do you feel about climbing through basement windows?"

"What?"

"Rob will be home tomorrow, but I usually do laundry on Thursday. He never comes down into the basement when I'm doing laundry. Would it turn you on to fuck me with Rob right upstairs over our heads?"

"Are you serious?"

"You betcha lover."

"Okay then; I'll do it."

"I'll unlock the window on the north east end and be waiting."

I sat there stunned and outraged to my very core. Stunned because my wife of ten years was fucking our next door neighbor. Outraged because he could have her ass anytime he wanted it because she never got tired of giving it to him, but I couldn't have it? And from the sound of it she had been doing it for some time. Where the hell had I been? I thought Beth loved me and that we had a solid marriage. How could I have been so wrong? She was going to drug me so she could fuck him at the Halloween party? Why? What was so special about the party? They were obviously managing to get it done at other times. And who the hell was Hal?

The sound of the garage door starting to run pulled me away from what I was watching and I headed upstairs and as I climbed the stairs, I was trying to make up my mind as to what to do. Confront or wait. I decided to wait. I wanted to know more. I wasn't interested in watching Beth cheating on me, but I did want to hear what was said. I wanted to know how long it had been going on and I wanted to know why.

The hardest part for me was going to be trying to act normal around Beth. We were through as far as the marriage was concerned, but she didn't need to know that until after I'd taken some steps to protect myself. We didn't live in one of those states where no fault divorces were the only way you could go and what I already had on DVD would make a divorce with adultery as grounds a slam dunk, but a court would still be making the decisions on asset distribution and I needed to make sure that Beth wasn't rewarded for her treachery.

Also, I needed more information that I might be able to use in taking my revenge on Jim. He was going to pay for fucking my wife in my house. Part of the revenge would be seeing to it that Carol, his wife, got a copy of the DVD, but that alone wouldn't satisfy my need to hurt him physically. I just needed to make it happen without putting me in jail.

~~***~~

Beth came in the door from the garage carrying two bags of groceries and she set them on the table and came over, put her arms around me and kissed me.

"I'm glad you're home baby. I hate waking up and not having you there beside me."

"Yeah, right," I thought as I wondered when she had given up on our marriage and why. And she had given it up and she should have known it. She knew my views on fidelity. My parents had split up because of my mom cheating on my dad. She had remarried and that marriage had failed when her new husband cheated on her. Beth had to know what the outcome was going to be if I caught her cheating on me. Apparently she didn't care.

"I stopped at the store on the way home because I needed bleach for when I do the laundry tonight and while I was there I decided to pick up the stuff to make you the stir fry you like so much. Go sit down and relax while I make dinner."

As I headed for the living room I thought about what was going to happen after dinner. The mention of bleach reminded me of what was going to take place in the basement later on in the evening. I had a decision to make. I always made love to Beth when coming home from a trip. Not to do it would probably raise questions in her mind and besides, when I dropped the hammer on her God alone knew when I would get laid again so even though she was a cheating whore, I was going to take what I could get while I could get it. The decision I had to make was whether to send her to the basement to give Jim sloppy seconds or have to take them myself after Jim paid her his visit.

It turned out that Beth got to make that decision for me. I tried to get something going after dinner, but she put me off.

"I need to get the laundry done honey and if we start playing I'll never break loose from you to get it done. I'll take good care of you when we go to bed. I promise."

From the way she was smiling at me when she said it, I got the impression – from what I now knew – that she was looking forward to giving me sloppy seconds. I wondered how many times she had already done it which thought pulled something out of my mind. Our love making, or fucking as I was now looking at it, included a lot of oral. Had the bitch let me eat her before cleaning up after Jim's visits? I was not thinking good thoughts as Beth went down to the basement to do the laundry. I would know what went on because of the camera in the basement, but I sure would have liked to hear what was being said that night instead of having to wait until I could get to the recorder.

I decided to tell Beth I was going into work late because of a dentist's appointment so I could check the recorder after Beth left for work. I had to fight the urge to quietly sneak outside and peek in the basement window, but I knew I couldn't risk being seen. I couldn't let them know that I knew about them. I debated doing a few things that might make them think I was going to come down into the basement, but then I decided that I needed to know what they talked about more than I needed the satisfaction of disrupting what they were doing. I needed to know more about this drugging that was supposed to take place.

I couldn't get interested in anything on TV and the book I picked up couldn't hold my attention either. I finally headed into the den and got on the computer, but that didn't do me any good either because all I could think of was what had taken place on the desk while I was gone.

Two hours after Beth had disappeared into the basement she came up and told me that she was going to take a quick shower and then:

"I'm going to rock your world baby."

I was surprised. I'd thought for sure that she was going to give me sloppy seconds. When she came out of the shower and got in bed with me she spread herself wide and said:

"Eat me lover. I got so wet in anticipation that I'm more than ready."

I would have found some reason to refuse if she hadn't showered, but since she had I bent to the task. As I munched I noticed a little redness around her asshole and it almost pissed me off enough to stop what I was doing and get up and go to the spare bedroom. But only almost. When I kicked her ass out it might be a long time before I'd get laid again so I needed to get what I could while I could. It wasn't as if I craved her ass anyway. Beth would let me have her butt occasionally when she had been drinking and was in a good mood, but she claimed she hated it so I didn't push all that hard for it. Face it; the main reason I wanted it was because she wouldn't give it to me very often. I ate Beth to an orgasm and then I moved up and fucked her. I didn't make love to her; I fucked her and there is a difference. I came; we snuggled up and went to sleep.

In the morning, Beth woke me up with a blow job and when I was awake and as hard as I was going to get, Beth moved over me and rode me cowgirl until we both got off. I had to wonder about that because we almost never had sex in the morning and when we did it was usually me who started it. Was she feeling guilty over what she planned to do to me at the party and was trying to make herself feel less guilty? I'd probably never know.

When we finished she kissed me and said, "Time to get up and get going. Got to get out and earn our daily bread."

"I'm going into work late this morning. I have a dentist appointment at nine."

"Something wrong?"

"No, just my regular checkup and cleaning."

As soon as Beth's car backed down the drive, I went down into the basement to see what the recorder had for me. I watched as Beth went over and unlocked the basement window and then go over and begin sorting things and loading them into the washer. I watched as Jim came in the window and I watched as he sat on the dryer and Beth sucked his cock. I watched him bend Beth over the washing machine and fuck her from behind. I watched as she sucked him hard again and then got up on the washer and gave him her ass. When the washer went into the spin cycle I almost wished I were Jim so I could feel the sensations that he must have been feeling, but the worst of it was not the watching – it was the listening. Jim had just finished fucking her bent over the washer and as he eased out of her cunt he said:

"You going to fuck dickwad tonight?"

"Hell yes. I really get off on letting him have seconds."

"Sloppy seconds?"

"Just a little."

"What do you mean just a little?"

"He always eats me before we make love and if I still had all that you shoot still in me he would likely catch on. What I do is take a spoonful of your stuff out of me and then I shower and douche and put the spoonful back in me. God, but it is such a turn on for me knowing that he is tasting you and then knowing that his little dick is sliding around in what little of you that I do have in me."

"I wish you would give him the full experience some day."

"Maybe after the party. He will be so groggy that he probably won't notice."

"You have the timing figured out yet?"

"It will depend on how quick the drugs knock Rob out. I figure the party will start breaking up around ten-thirty or eleven. If Rob is out by then we can get started."

As I shut off the unit, my hand was trembling because of the anger surging through me. The bitch had deliberately fed me her asshole lover's cum. It was at that moment that my anger and outrage turned into full blown burning hatred. I knew I was going to have my work cut out for me as I tried to hide what I was feeling from Beth.

I managed to get through the evening without revealing anything to Beth although she might have wondered why I didn't try to screw her that night. I told her I pulled a muscle in my back at work and she seemed to buy it.

The next day was spent getting the house ready for the party and then at seven the guests began arriving. First to show up was Jim and his wife Carol. I wondered how that was going to work out. Were they going to leave and then Jim would sneak back or maybe she was going to get drugged also. Ten minutes after Jim got there Beth brought me my first drink. I pretended to take a sip and when Beth didn't see me make a face at the taste she smiled and went to talk to some of our guests.

Beth brought me nine drinks that night, but I didn't drink any of them although I did start acting like I was taking on a load after the third. By the time Beth gave me the ninth I was slurring my words and staggering.

"Poor baby," she said, "I think you have had too much to drink. I think you should lie down for a bit. Let me help you up to bed."

I let her lead me down the hall, but she surprised me by taking me into the guest bedroom. I pretended not to notice and got down on the bed. She left me there and went back to the party. I looked at the bedside clock and saw that it was just after ten. If I had it figured right she would be back to check on me in about twenty minutes. She was back in fifteen.

"You okay baby?"

I pretended to be out. She shook me a couple of times and I didn't respond. She put her mouth down by my ear and loudly said:

"Are you okay Rob?"

"I didn't move.

"Thank you God," she said and left the room.

Ten minutes later it was Jim. He shook me while saying, "Rob? Rob?" and I acted like I was totally out of it and then I heard Beth ask:

"What do you think?"

Jim laughed and said, "He is so far out of it he may not wake up until sometime late tomorrow afternoon."

"Good. Most of the guests have left and we can get started."

I gave it fifteen minutes and then I cracked the door open enough to see out. The master bedroom was just across the hall and the door was open. What I saw almost made me want to rush into the room and start kicking ass and taking manes, but I wisely didn't. No fucking way that I wouldn't have ended up in the hospital if I tried. I can give a pretty good account of myself in a scrap, but no way I could handle six or eight guys. Beth was being gangbanged. She had a cock in her ass, a cock in her cunt and one in her mouth. All thoughts of burning Jim by showing his wife the video I had of Jim fucking Beth went out the window. Carol was next to Beth on the bed and she was being spit roasted.

Standing around and waiting for an open hole were three other guys that I could see. There might have been more, but if so they were off to the side where I couldn't see. I knew most of the assholes I could see. Four were neighbors and two of them worked with me. I closed the door and then shook my head in disgust. I walked over to the window, opened it and climbed out. I walked down to the end of the block and walked up to a parked car. The passenger window came down and I looked in as I said:

"Anything else I need to do?"

"No. We have it all bagged and tagged. When we get the report from the lab we will move on it. Just be careful and don't do anything silly that might get you locked up. No taking the law into your own hands stuff."

"Don't worry. I won't do anything that might give them a chance to lessen the hammer blow that is coming."

"We should have the proof by noon on Monday. I'll give you a call," Detective Sergeant Thomas Callings said as he rolled up the window and his partner started the car.

I went back to the house, went back through the window and settled in for a long night. As I laid there, I though back on what I had done on Friday afternoon. I'd gone to the City and County building and asked for the district attorney. They gave me to an Assistant District Attorney and I played him the video of Jim and Beth talking about drugging me. He called Detective Callings and we set things up so that Callings could come to the party as a friend of mine. Callings would observe Beth and Jim handing me drinks and then I would pass them to him and he would bag and tag them and then turn them over to a lab. When the lab report came back showing that the drinks were laced with drugs, Beth and Jim would be arrested.

While Beth was in jail, I would divorce her cheating ass and she wouldn't get a fucking thing as far as asset distribution was concerned. I think I fell asleep with a smile on my face.

The next day I acted like I had the hangover to end all hangovers and Beth stayed clear of me until late afternoon when I started acting human again. As we ate dinner Beth said:

"You over did it a bit last night."

"I don't understand it. I didn't think I drank that much, but given the way I felt when I woke up I must have."

"You left me hanging."

"I did? How?"

"You know how horny I get when I drink. I was expecting you to take care of my itch after the party. You will have your work cut out for you tonight."

"I'm afraid I'll have to let you down again. The way I feel right now, any exertion at all would probably kill me. I'll do my best to recover in time for tomorrow night."

After seeing what I saw the previous night there was no fucking way I was going to let my dick anywhere near her fucking cunt. I'd probably not even be able to feel the sides.

~~***~~

Monday at eleven I got a call from Callings. "The lab report came back positive. We are getting the warrants even as we speak. Would you like to be there when we do it?"

"Yes and no. Do Beth where she works, but do Case at his home around six tonight. That way I can be on my porch watching as you take him away."

Before I left work I told my boss that I'd caught my wife cheating and I was going to need to take a couple of days off to take care of things. Then I told him that two of the men she cheated with were coworkers and when I got done with taking care of Beth, I'd get to them so he should be prepared to lose Fred and Alvin to sick leave for a while. He asked if I was sure and I told him I had it on tape. When I got back to work three days later both were gone. My boss reasoned that if my coworkers could have done something like that then they were untrustworthy in other areas also and so he did some checking. Alvin was fired for cheating on his expense accounts and Fred, by then aware that I knew about him, had resigned and left town.

I was sitting on the porch and thinking of Beth's phone call to me when the police car pulled up in front of Jim's house. As the police walked up to Jim's front door, I rolled over in my head the conversation I'd had with Beth.

"Rob honey...I don't know what is going on, but I'm in jail. They say it has something to do with drugs. I don't do drugs. There has to be some mistake. They won't let me go until I go in front of a judge. What do I do Rob?"

"Well Beth, I've always heard it said that you shouldn't do the crime if you can't do the time," and I hung up on her.

Next door the police were putting the cuffs on Jim and as they walked him to the police car he looked over at me and I waved 'bye-bye' at him. Carol was on the porch and she saw me do it. When the police car pulled away she came over.

"I saw you wave at Jimmy. Do you know what is going on?"

"I guess it is against the law to drug somebody."

"What does that mean?"

"It means that you should have waited until I was out of town to have your gangbang instead of drugging me and stuffing me into the spare bedroom to get me out of the way."

I saw understanding register on her face. "You bastard! You are responsible for this."

"No Carol, you, your husband and Beth are the ones responsible. I don't recall raising my hand and saying 'pick me' when the question 'Anyone here want to be drugged?' was asked."

"He could go to prison."

"Yes he could and that is what I'm hoping for. Maybe he and Beth can share a cell."

"Beth?"

"She was arrested at work around four this afternoon."

"You could do that to your own wife? What kind of man are you?"

"A very pissed off one. Did any of you assholes bother to find out if I was allergic to the shit you tried to feed me? What if I had gone into shock and died while you were in my bedroom fucking and sucking every cock you could get your hands on. You, your husband and my cheating whore of a wife are damned lucky I don't own a gun or the police would have been here for me for committing multiple murders. Now, why don't you get your slutty whorish ass off my front porch?"

She left and halfway to her house she turned and gave me the finger. I just laughed at her and blew her a kiss. I finished my beer, went into the basement and got busy. By noon the next day, a copy of the video of the gangbang was on the way to the wives and girlfriends of all the men who took part. Except for one. I just couldn't bring myself to send one to her.

~~***~~

At ten the next morning, I got a call from the Public Defender's office. An attorney named Andrew Morris was representing Beth and he called me to tell me that her bail had been set at twenty-five thousand and if I would make the necessary arrangements she could be home that afternoon. I think he was shocked when I laughed at him and told him that she could sit in jail and rot for all I cared and then I hung up on him.

As soon as I hung up, I realized that I hadn't thought things through. Beth had her checkbook and credit cards. Once she knew I wasn't going to help she could get cash advances and drain the checking account to bail herself out. I quickly called the credit card companies and cancelled all of our cards and requested new ones. It would take maybe a week to get the new ones, but I would be able to get by until they arrived. Then I rushed to the bank and cleaned out all of our accounts and closed them.

I stopped and had dinner at the Outback Steak House and then I went on home. I spent the next morning going through the house and gathering up everything of Beth's that I could find. I packed it all in boxes and garage bags and moved it out into the garage. The locksmith showed up at eleven and changed all the house locks.

I had a three-fifteen appointment with an attorney to get the divorce going and I debated going out for lunch and then going to my appointment or just making a sandwich. Before I could make the decision the doorbell rang and when I opened the door I saw Jim standing there.

"You owe me twenty-five hundred dollars cocksucker and I want it now."

"Why do I owe you twenty-five hundred dollars?"

"Because that is the ten percent I had to put up to go your wife's bail."

"Well gosh Jim, I certainly want to see that you get what you have coming. Come on in."

He stepped into the house and I hit him as hard as I could right in the face. I must have broken his nose because there was blood everywhere. He staggered and I hit him again as I said:

"I'm damned sure going to see that you get what I owe you."

I hit him a third time and he slumped to the floor. I proceeded to tire out my foot kicking him in the head, ribs and crotch. Then I got on the phone and called the police station and asked for Detective Callings. When he came on the line I said:

"Case made bail and came after me. He said he was going to make me pay for what I did to him. He pushed his way into my house and I had to defend myself. What should I do?"

"You okay?"

"Yes. A little shaken up, but okay."

"Where is Case?"

"Lying on my floor. He doesn't look too good."

"I'll get a car to you right away."

Three minutes later a squad car pulled up and when the officers looked at Jim, they called for an ambulance. As Jim was being carried out, Carol came over and said:

"What the fuck have you done now?"

"Just defended myself."

"Bullshit Rob. He didn't come over to fight you. He just wanted the money he put up for Beth's bail."

"And he really thought I'd give it to him? She's your whore now. I washed my hands of her. Anything you do for her is between you and her. If you know where she is you need to call her and tell her to get in touch with me to make arrangements to get her things."

"She said she was going into work and explain why she wasn't there before coming home."

"Coming home? She doesn't live here anymore. But if she is coming, I'll leave the garage door open so she can get her stuff. Tell her anything still here come trash pick-up day will go out on the curb with the rest of the garbage."

"You can't mean that."

"Of course I mean it. Now if you will excuse me I have some blood I need to clean off my floor."

That afternoon after giving the attorney all the video that I had on what Beth had been doing, I told him about Jim's visit and he said that along with filing the paperwork for the divorce, he would get a restraining order against Jim and Beth.

"Have to include her. If she was willing to drug you no telling what else she might do."

I found Beth sitting in her car on our driveway when I got home. I parked in the street so I wouldn't block her and keep her from leaving. I could see that she was pissed as she walked up to me and when she got close she said:

"You bastard!" As she went to swing at me. I caught her wrist and squeezed hard and didn't let go until she said "That hurts. Let go." I let go and got ready to grab her if she tried it again, but she didn't.

"Why did you hang up on me when I called you from the jail and why wouldn't you come down and bail me out. And why can't I get in the house?"

"Let's take the last one first. You can't get in the house because I don't want you there and I had the locks changed. Next, I didn't go your bail because I hoped that you would rot in that jail. Finally, I hung up on you because I was pissed at what you did to me that put you in jail."

"What I did to you? I didn't do anything to you."

"That's true, but you tried."

"Tried what?"

"To drug me so I would sleep through your gangbang."

"Have you been drinking Rob? You aren't making any sense."

"Give it up Beth. I have you and Jim on tape planning what you were going to do to get me out of the way. I have your laundry night fucks on the washing machine on DVD and I have your Gangbang on

DVD. Face it Beth, your cheating ass is busted. Your clothes and other things are in the garage. You need to get them out by next trash pick-up day or they will go out on the curb with the rest of the garbage."

I walked away from her toward the house as she said, "Wait Rob. We have to talk about this."

"Tell you what Beth. I'll send you a copy of what I gave the divorce lawyer and after you watch it you still think we should talk give me a call."

"Divorce? I don't want a divorce Rob."

"Maybe not Beth, but you are going to get one just the same."

I unlocked the front door, went into the house and locked the door behind me.

~~***~~

When Jim was released from the hospital he went in front of a judge with the new charges against him and the judge revoked his bail and then denied bail on the new charges. He will have to sit in jail until his trial. Beth moved in with Carol and I saw her on most days, but never had anything to do with her. She tried to talk to me a couple of times even after I sent her copies of the DVD showing what she had done, but I managed to avoid her except for one time when she caught me getting out of my car in the driveway.

"You have to talk to me honey. You don't understand and I need to explain things."

"Of course I understand Beth. I understand that the ass you rationed out to me was Jim's anytime that he wanted it. I understand what a turn on it was for you to fuck Jim on my desk in the den and I understand the charge you got out of fucking Jim on the washing machine with me being right upstairs over you. You are the one who doesn't understand. You don't understand how disgusted I am with you and what you did. Get away from me Beth and stay the fuck away from me."

When Beth's trial came up she pled not guilty, but the security system footage was damning and she was found guilty on all charges and was sentenced to a year and a day. While she was doing her time, the divorce became final. All she got in the distribution of assets was ten percent of the value of the house at the time of divorce. I had the house appraised and then took out a second mortgage for ten percent of the appraised value and then opened a savings account in Beth's name and put the money in her account. That hopefully put an end to her being in my life.

Jim was found guilty on all charges, both in connection with the attempted doping and attacking me in my home. Because he was the one who obtained the drugs, he got three to five on the doping charges and a year on what happened at my house.

I was in the court for his sentencing and Carol came up to me and said:

"I hope you are happy now."

"Not really. I was hoping that he would get at least ten years."

"Asshole!" she snarled. "Whorish cunt," I said with a smile and then I went back to work.

The packages I sent out to the wives and girlfriends of the gangbang participants caused six divorces and two break ups of engaged couples and two of the guys tried to get even with me for causing their problems. One ended up in the hospital and the other almost beat me until I picked up a rock and smashed him in the head with it. I left him lying behind a dumpster and I don't know what happened to him.

~~***~~

Now here I was six months later with Angie bringing it all back to me.

"How did you find out what happened? I went out of my way to keep it from you."

"I still want to know why you let Gary slide while you went after the others."

"Oh come on Angie, you have to know the answer to that. Remember that old Ford Galaxy 500 station wagon of my dad's with the air mattress in the back? Remember Steven's Point?"

"God no. A girl never forgets her first time. You let Gary slide because of me?"

"A guy never forgets his first time either. I didn't want to see you hurt. How did you find out?"

"Gary told me."

"He told you? You have one of those open marriages I've been hearing about?"

"Not hardly. He got to feeling guilty and he confessed to me and begged me to forgive him. Since it was partially my fault I ended up forgiving him."

"Partially your fault?"

"Gary has always wanted to try anal sex and I would never let him. I couldn't make the party because my mom was in the hospital so Gary went alone. He didn't go there to screw Beth. He was just going to have a couple of drinks and then leave. A show of the flag so to speak. You know, put in an appearance to show we appreciated being thought of when guest list was made up. Anyway, when he was ready to leave he went looking for you and Beth to say goodbye and thank you for inviting us. He couldn't find you, but he did find Beth. When he found her, she was naked and being used by three guys. The guy in her butt finished and when he pulled out, Beth pulled her mouth off the guy in front of her and said:

"Somebody hurry and get in my ass."

Another guy stepped up and pushed in her. Gary had always wanted to try anal sex and Beth was giving it up so Gary undressed and the next time her ass was open he stepped up and took it. He liked it. He liked it enough to let her suck him hard again so he could have another shot at it. He did her ass three times before leaving and would have gone a fourth if he could have gotten it up again.

"On the drive home he started feeling guilty. He was upset for cheating on me and he was upset because he betrayed your friendship. It ate at him all day Sunday and Sunday evening he confessed. He was going to confess to you also, but I wouldn't let him."

"You wouldn't let him?"

"A minute ago you asked if I had an open marriage. Well, I didn't know but that you and Beth had one. Even if you did have one and Gary confessed it would still leave the thought in your mind that Gary didn't know and since he didn't know what he did was stab you in the back. I convinced him that the best course was to keep quiet and wait and see if you and Beth would invite him back for more or if nothing ever came of it. Of course days later when Beth was hauled off to jail we knew that you didn't have an open marriage. Gary still wanted to confess, but I still wouldn't let him."

"Why not?"

"Because you would have most likely ended your friendship with him and that would mean that by association you would have ended your friendship with me."

"Never Angie. I have too many good memories of our time together."

"I have those same memories Rob, but one of them was not so good. In a way it is ironic that you fucking my butt is what led to Gary's fucking Beth's."

"How so?"

"You never figured out why I broke up with you?"

"No. I was crushed that the girl I wanted to marry wouldn't even talk to me anymore. I tried for months to get you to talk to me and you never would so I finally put it behind me and got on with my life."

"You never associated what we did the last time we were together with my not talking to you?"

"No I didn't."

"It was the night you talked me into having anal sex. It hurt like hell and I kept telling you to stop and you ignored me. It got to the point where it hurt so bad that I was screaming at you to stop and you never did until you got your rocks off. I was so pissed at you when you took me home that I swore I would never have anything to do with you ever again. I eventually got over it, but by the time I was ready to talk to you it was too late and you were already with Beth. I kept waiting for the two of you to break up so we could get back together, but it never happened."

"I never knew. I'm sorry about the anal thing. The guys all told me that it hurt at first, but that if you stayed with it the girl eventually got into it. It probably sounds stupid now, but I was so into it I really thought those later screams were screams of pleasure."

"Well they weren't. Anyway, after that session with you I swore that I would never do anal again so Gary never got any and that's what led him into fucking Beth when he got a chance to finally do anal."

She was silent for a bit and then she said, "You never had any urge to get some revenge on Gary?"

"Human nature being what it is of course I've wanted to get back at him, but I couldn't find a way that wouldn't let you know why and I didn't want to hurt you."

"What if I gave you a way that wouldn't hurt me?"

"Why would you do that?"

"Revenge. I did forgive Gary, but it was forgiveness with a price. I told him I wouldn't throw his ass out, but that he owed me one."

"Owes you one?"

"I told him that someday I might want to try on a different guy and if that day ever came and I did take advantage of it he wasn't to bitch about it. He would have to chalk it up to our being even."

"Are you suggesting what I think you are?"

"You betcha!"

"This sucks!"

"Why?"

"I just kicked a woman to the curb for cheating on me. If I take you up on your offer I'll be cheating with you behind your husband's back and that would make me no better than Beth."

"You are looking at it the wrong way."

"How so?"

"You aren't cheating with me behind Gary's back. Gary knows I'm going to fuck some guy to get even with him so I'm not cheating and therefore you aren't cheating."

"Are you sure that you aren't a lawyer?"

"It gets better. I want you to screw me in my butt. It would be the most fitting revenge I could think of. Giving you what I won't give him."

"You just said that you hated it and would never do it again."

"I have some girl friends who like it and say that it is great if it is done right. How about it? Have you learned to do it right since our last time?"

"I thought you said you were trying to keep me friends with Gary. That won't be likely once he finds out."

"He won't find out unless you tell him. I'm going to tell him that we are even, but I'm not going to tell him who I got even with or what I did to get even."

"It is very tempting Angie, but I don't think I can do it. I want to; God knows I want to, but I would still be screwing another man's wife behind his back. That's just not me Angie. I can be friends with Gary. Now that I know the story and that he hadn't been fucking the slut all along like the others I can cut him some slack. I will say this. If you and Gary ever break up you have my number."

~~***~~

A week later I was kicking myself for not taking Angie up on her offer. I hadn't been laid in months and I was hurting. I was thinking of calling around to see if anyone knew of a good escort service that had girls who 'would go the extra mile' if you take my meaning when the answer to my problem rang my doorbell.

When I opened the door I found Carol standing there. Remembering the acrimonious parting of our last meeting, I just stood there and looked at her without saying a word. She looked me in the eye and said:

"The whorish cunt wants to ask the asshole for a favor."

"And that would be?"

"I need to get laid and I'm hoping that by now you do too."

"Why me? Why not one of the herd that you and Beth were taking care of?"

"I don't like any of them and I was only there because Jim was making me do it."

"Making you do it?"

"I don't want to talk out here on the porch. Let me come inside, fuck me and then I'll tell you the whole sad story."

I was just a tad leery of it and I looked around to see if anyone else was lurking about. Seeing no one and being more than a little curious I stepped aside and let her come in. She walked straight by me and headed for the bedroom shedding clothes as she went.

I did have to admit that the way her ass moved as she walked toward my bed in her high heels had my cock straining my pants. I started unzipping as I followed along behind her. She laid down on the bed, spread her legs wide and said:

"I don't need any stinking foreplay. Just do it!"

I hadn't gotten a real good look at her on the DVD of the gangbang because of all the male bodies blocking the view, but there wasn't anything blocking my view now and what I was looking at was sex personified. You would never know it from the way she dressed, but Carol had a body that was made for male appreciation. And she had a shaved pussy. I had tried to get Beth to shave hers, but she never would. I got on the bed and my face went for that bald crotch.

"I don't want foreplay," she said.

"Don't care what you want. My bedroom, my rules, and one of my rules is that a shaven pussy has to be eaten before it gets fucked."

It was an exhausting evening. I ate her until she screamed at me to fuck her and then I fucked her. She went down on me and got me up and I did her doggie. We went moved into a sixty-nine and she rode me cowgirl and then followed it up with a blow job that just couldn't get me up no matter how hard she tried.

"If I'm still here in the morning do you think you might be rested up enough to go again?"

"I would certainly hope so."

"Not going to kick me out?"

"Shit girl. I may never let you leave."

"Promises, promises. All I ever get is promises."

We fell asleep together and I slept good for the first time in a long while. I woke up in the morning with a female hand fondling my cock and it responded. When I was hard, Carol mounted me and rode me cowgirl until we both got off. We showered and then I took her out to breakfast. Over pancakes and bacon I reminded her that she was supposed to tell me a story.

"It isn't pretty."

"Maybe not, but you said you would tell me all about it if I laid you. I did my part and now you have to do yours."

"I was an inexperienced young girl working as a waitress in a small café when Jim came in for lunch one day. I felt all tingly inside when I first saw him and he must have liked what he saw in me because he came back for breakfast and lunch the next day. He asked me out and I accepted and over the course of the next month he seduced me and got my cherry. I took to sex like a moth to a flame. I became Jim's steady girl and for six months we lived together.

"Then one day he told me that he needed me to help him out with a business deal. He wanted me to party with three guys that he wanted to get on the good side of. I told him no way so he drugged me and gave me to them anyway. The three used me for the entire weekend and I won't lie; they got me going and they kept me going with sex and more drugs. The problem is that they were black and I'm from a family that is one hundred percent racist. I was filmed doing things with those black men that would have made my mother's hair fall out and looking at the film after Jim had edited it you would think that I was doing it all willingly and to be honest, for the most part I was because once they got my body going I did get into it.

"Sunday night Jim picked me up and took me back to our place and I hit the bed and slept for almost twenty-four hours. When I woke up I started to pack and when Jim asked me where I thought I was going I told him that I was going as far away from him as I could get. He laughed and told me that I wasn't going anywhere; that I was his personal whore and I needed to get used to the idea. I told him to fuck off and die and that's when he showed me the tape he had of me and the black guys. He told me to behave or my parents and all of my other living relatives would get their own personal copy of the tape. I couldn't let my family see that tape. None of them would ever talk to me again.

"Over the next year he used me to sweeten some of the deals he made. He only taped me when he had me doing black guys and he held those tapes over my head to keep me in line."

"If he was that big of an asshole why did you marry him?"

"We aren't married. He just told everyone that we were."

"You should have been glad to see him go to jail so why were you always giving me a ration of shit for trying to send him there?"

"Because of the tapes he has of me. I don't know where they are and with him in jail he has relatives who are going to show up some day to grab his stuff. If they find the tapes, or worse yet Jim tells them where they are I'll never get free. My best hope was for him not to go to jail and hope that he slipped up and gave me some idea of where he has them. I've spent every day he is in jail looking for them with no luck. I'm running out of time."

"Running out of time?"

"I had a call from Jim's brother. He is going to be here in two weeks. He told me to be sure I was here when he gets here. He said we had lots to talk about. I'm guessing he knows where the tapes are and is planning on picking up where Jim left off."

"Are you sure that the tapes are at the house?"

"Jim is one of those guys who likes to keep things close. I don't know what the fuck I'm going to do."

"Sure you do. We are going to find those tapes, films or whatever before Jim's brother gets here."

"We?"

"Got to keep you happy girl so you'll stay close to my bed."

"Find me those tapes and I'll never leave it."

We finished breakfast and went back to the house. Carol was silent most of the way and we were almost there when she said:

"He drugged Beth too you know."

"I don't believe it. She wasn't drugged that night."

"No, but he did drug her and filmed her pulling a train. Told her she would fuck him or for him whenever he wanted or you would get the tape."

"When did it happen?"

Six, maybe seven months ago. You were on one of your business trips and Jim invited Beth over to have dinner with us. He drugged her and then called a bunch of guys to come over and do her. She really didn't have a chance Rob. When it was over she was scared to death you would find out."

"Bullshit! Beth knew me better than that. She could have told me and I would have gone over and beat on Jim like a drum until he gave me the tapes. You can't blackmail someone who won't cooperate. Granted that Beth's situation was way different than yours, but Beth knew that I would fight for her. She knew if she told me she was drugged I'd believe it and go after Jim. She went along because she wanted to go along."

"You can't know that."

"Remind me to show you the tapes I have of Jim and her sometime. She was holding onto the "He drugged me and blackmailed me" so she could use it as a 'get out of jail free' card if I ever caught her."

When we got back to my place, I went out into the garage and got some tools and then went over to her place.

"Are there any rooms where Jim spent a lot of time?"

"Just the den and the basement."

We went into the den and I saw that it was paneled.

"Jim owns the house right? It's not leased or rented?"

"No. He owns it."

"Good. We don't have to worry about damage."

I went over the walls with my stud finder and found three places that did not seem to read right. I took my crow bar and started ripping down the paneling over the questionable areas. There was nothing behind the first one, but as soon as I put the crowbar behind the edge of the paneling over the second section, it popped open revealing a cavity between the wall studs. It was packed with video tapes, CDs and DVDs. I told Carol to find a box to put it all in and while she was gone I went over to the third questionable area. Again, as soon as I put the crowbar behind the edge of the paneling it popped open to reveal a cavity between the wall studs only this one was packed with money. Carol came back into the room with a box and I said:

"Looks like I found you some running money."

She came over and looked and said, "Oh my God. How much is there?"

"Don't know. We can count it as we take it out."

She left the room and came back with a suitcase. There was sixty-seven thousand dollars in hundreds and fifties, a small bag that held diamonds and twenty-six gold coins.

"What are we going to do with it" Carol asked.

"We?"

"Over breakfast you did tell me that we were in this together."

I reached over and picked up six of the gold coins and said, "I have always wanted to have some gold. As for the rest of it we can get you a safe deposit box at the bank. Do you have a checking account?"

"No. Jim gave me three hundred a week to run the house. Buy groceries and such, gas for the car and stuff like that. I kept it in my purse. He didn't want me to have too much. It might tempt me to run."

"Is the car yours?"

"No. It belongs to Jim."

"It's yours now. I'm pretty sure that the title is here somewhere in the house. When we find it I'll fake Jim's signature and sign it over to you. Next question. Is there anything in the house that you want? If so we need to get it out of here before Jim's brother gets here."

"There is some stuff."

"Go through the house and make a list and we will get it out of here and put it in storage. Since he fucked my wife I figure that he owes me so I'm going to go through his stuff and see if there is anything that I want."

We carried the money and the tapes over to my house and went through them. There were six with Beth's name on them and fourteen with Carol's and we set them aside. I started to go through the rest of them to make sure that Carol wasn't on any of them and she said:

"Why bother. If I'm on any of them I'm going to destroy them so let's just destroy all of them and be done with it."

"Maybe after I go through them. I want to see who else I know that he might have been blackmailing so I can let them know they are free of him."

"You really are a decent guy aren't you?"

"I try."

I found four women that I knew on the tapes and I set them aside and then we destroyed all the other tapes, CDs and DVDs. I had Carol call the four women and tell them that she had found the blackmail material and then ask them if they wanted the evidence or just wanted her to destroy it. All four of them said to just destroy the stuff and they thanked Carol for getting rid of the axe that been hanging over their heads. I cheated and held onto one of them. I'd had the hots for her all the way through high school and had tried to hook up with her several times when we were in college, but she always turned me down. Seeing her on three of the tapes gave me one hell of a hard on so I decided to keep one for myself without letting Carol know that I'd done it. We destroyed all the material except those that had Beth on them. Those I wanted to look at before destroying them.

"Now what?" Carol asked.

"What do you mean?"

"What do we do now?"

"You can do whatever you want. You are free of Jim and you have plenty of money for a new start."

"Trying to get rid of me already?"

I looked at her with a "What?" expression on my face and after a couple of seconds she said:

"Earlier you told me that you would help me to keep me happy enough to stay close to your bed and I told you if you helped me find the stuff I'd never leave it. Did you not mean what you said, because I did mean what I said."

I just stared at her and she laughed and said, "Race you to the bedroom."

~~***~~

Over the next three days we moved everything out of Jim's house that we wanted. Most of it went into storage, but all of Carol's clothes ended up in my house. We also went to my bank and opened checking and savings accounts for Carol and rented her a safe deposit box for the bulk of the cash, diamonds and gold coins. Most of the cash had to go into the deposit box because deposits of ten grand or more brought scrutiny from the feds.

I found the title to Jim's car in his desk and I signed Jim's name to it and gave Carol a bill of sale for the car also with Jim's name signed to it. Carol of course moved in with me and she left no forwarding address when she left Jim's house so Jim's brother had no way of finding her. Not that it would have done him any good if he had.

I wondered what he thought when he went into the house and found it pretty much empty. I also wondered how Jim took it when he was told about the almost empty house and what his brother had found in the den. I would have loved to have seen his face when he found out that all of his blackmail material, his money and Carol were gone.

I watched all the tapes that had Beth's name on them and they weren't half bad as far as porn went, but you could see that Beth was enjoying the hell out of it. Carol kept trying to tell me that I wasn't being fair; that once the guys got Beth wound up of course she got into it and enjoyed it. Carol kept telling me that I had to keep it in mind that everything was edited and that Beth's reluctance at the begging was edited out. Finally I got out the surveillance tapes that I had and showed them to Carol and after she saw them she never said another word about cutting Beth any slack.

~~***~~

Three months went by and Carol and I were living, for all practical purposes, as man and wife. I began thinking that I should make it real, but I hesitated to bring up the subject because I was afraid. Afraid of what might happen if I asked Carol to marry me and she said no.

I was comfortable being with Carol and I didn't want the relationship to end. I wasn't in love with her the way I had been in love with Beth and I knew it, but I had come to the opinion that love was highly overrated. I doubted that Carol loved me either, but we fit. We got along great. We made love three or four times a week and usually more than once. We went out and had fun. We shared the household chores and as I earlier mentioned, we were just like a married couple only without all the legal stuff. I did try to work myself up to broach the subject with her.

Carol was a lot more in tune with me than I expected. I was just about ready to bring it up over dinner one night, but before I could say a word she said:

"I have a feeling that I know what is on your mind and I was afraid that this day would come."

"Afraid? Why?"

"Because you are getting ready to talk permanence and I can't go there. At least I can't go there with you."

"I thought we had something good going."

"We do, but only because we haven't made it permanent."

"I don't understand."

"Only because it hasn't happened yet. I told you once that even though Jim blackmailed me into doing it I got into it once they got me up to speed. I enjoyed the hell out of it. I enjoyed it so much I want to do it again, but of my own free will. The problem is that you just are not the kind of man who would go along with it."

"You got that right."

"In fact, I'm not even sure that if I lived in my own place and we were just friends with benefits you would have anything to do with me if I did it and you found out."

"If that's the case why haven't you done it before now?"

"I don't know that I ever will, but the fact is that I want to and if the circumstances ever arise that would set it in place I'd do it. I'm not sure that you are even going to want me around now that you know."

"I'm not that narrow minded. No way I would ever ask you to leave because of something you might want to do some day. You just told me that you don't know if it will ever happen so let's just play it by ear and we will see about crossing that bridge if we ever come to it.

~***~

The next nine months went by with no big problems. Anyone looking at us would think that we were the perfect couple and for the most part we were. My life with Carol was pretty much the same as my life with Beth had been only without the marriage license. The only blight was that having been forewarned by Carol I was waiting for the other shoe to drop. She said that it might never happen, but she also said that if the right circumstances presented itself then she would.

Unfortunately, the situations where those circumstances could arise were plentiful. Once Carol was free of Jim, she found a job at an advertising agency and she would occasionally stop for drinks after work with the girls she worked with and she also had a night out with them every once in a while. Carol admitted that they got hit on a lot and that she occasionally danced with the guys that bought the girls drinks and she also admitted to being felt up a time or two.

She went to baby showers and bridal showers and there were Mary Kaye, Tupperware and Amway parties. I didn't expect that anything would happen at those events, but what was constantly on my mind was the way some women talked and acted when there were no men around. I could imagine certain things being talked up and maybe leading to something. Something like a bachelorette party where a male stripper is brought in and things get out of hand and he calls his buddies for backup.

My problem was that I had liked being married when Beth and I were together and I wanted to go back to being married. And Carol suited me, but Carol had also been honest with me. There would be no going behind my back the way Beth did, but because of that honesty Carol wouldn't marry me. What I had was a teeter-totter. On one end was my relationship with Carol that I got more and more comfortable with every day, on the other end was the knowledge that if the opportunity presented itself, Carol would follow through on having her gangbang and we would be through as a couple. Hell of a deal. Hang in there and hope while at the same time setting myself up for the possible train wreck.

~~***~~

Thursday at dinner Carol reminded me that she would be going to the bachelorette party for one of the girls she worked with and Friday at breakfast she told me she would probably be late and not to wait up for her so I was in bed asleep when she got home. When I got up at five for my Saturday morning golf date with Ben, Dave and Chuck, it was pouring down rain so I got back in bed and went back to sleep. About nine the phone rang and Carol rolled over and picked it up off of the bedside table.

"Hello?"

"Carol."

"Yes, he's here but he's asleep."

"No. I won't wake him up, but I'll take a message."

"I'll make sure he gets it."

"Bye."

She hung up the phone and I asked, "Who was that?"

"I didn't know you were awake."

"The phone woke me up. Who was it?"

"It was Beth. She wanted me to wake you up so she could talk to you."

"About what?"

"She didn't say. I think she was too surprised that it was me she was talking to. She asked me to give you a message. She wants to talk to you and she will call back at one."

"You should have told her not to bother. I don't want or need to talk to her."

"Not my place baby. That is something that you have to do yourself."

She nudged me and said, "Up lazy-bones; I feel the need for an IHOP breakfast."

"How about we stay here and indulge in some hot monkey sex?"

"Later. Right now my head hurts from last night. I don't want to do any bouncing around until the head feels a tad better. Come on lover; up and at 'em."

She got out of bed and headed for the shower. I debated following her, but I knew what that would lead to, but I'd been in the 'head hurting' condition a time or two myself so I didn't want to inflict any pain on her.

Over breakfast Carol said, "I wonder what Beth wants?"

"Doesn't much matter. She won't be getting it."

"Are you sure? You loved her deeply at one time and I know that she loves you. At least she did before you sent her to jail."

"That was then sweetie. This is now."

She changed the subject and started talking about going to Alicia's wedding the next weekend.

At one Beth called. She told me that she wanted to sit down with me and try to explain what happened and why. I told her that I wasn't at all interested in hearing about any of it.

"Please Rob, I need to do it. Maybe you don't need to hear it, but I need to say it."

Against my better judgment I agreed to meet her. I told her I would meet her at Bud's Bar at four. Beth was already there and sitting in a booth when I got there. She smiled when she saw me and started to get up, but figuring that she was planning on giving me a hug I motioned her to sit back down. I sat across from her and said:

"Your meeting Beth so get to it."

"Not even a hello Beth, how are you doing?"

"Let me make this absolutely clear Beth. When I was in court for your sentencing it was the last time I hoped that I would ever see you. I left the courtroom disappointed that you were only give a year and a day. I was hoping for five or even ten. Does that give you any idea where you stand with me? The only thing on my mind right now as far as you are concerned is my wondering what you are doing out of prison. It hasn't even been a year."

"I got time off for good behavior."

"You behaved? Too bad you couldn't have done that while we were married."

"That's what I needed to talk with you about. I didn't do it because I didn't love you Rob, because I do and I always have. Honest to God I do. I was doing what I did because I was being blackmailed."

"I know all about it Beth. Jim drugged you, got you gangbanged and filmed it and then he told you he would show me the film if you didn't do what he wanted."

"If you knew all that why have you been so hard on me?"

"Because it is all bullshit Beth and we both know it. Yes, you were drugged and gangbanged and yes you enjoyed it, but so what? You know me well enough to know what I would have done if you had told Jim to fuck off and die. You know damned well that I would have ripped his head off and shit down his neck if you would have told me what he did. You know me well enough to know that I would have stood behind you. You could have laughed at him and told him to start running because you were going to tell me what he'd done.

"No Beth, you liked what happened and you wanted to do it again and so you did. You did whatever Jim told you he wanted you to do because you wanted to do it and I have the proof of that Beth. I sent you a copies of the videos I had Beth. Have you forgotten what they showed?"

"I never watched them."

"You should have. It would have saved you a trip to this meeting. They showed Jim fucking you on my desk in the den to mark his territory as he called it. Remember that Beth? He asked you if there was any chance that he could fuck you again before the party. Remember that Beth? You invited him to climb in the basement window so he could fuck you. You invited him. There was no "You will let me in the basement window so I can fuck you while Rob is upstairs and you will do it if you know what is good for you. There was no blackmail there Beth. None at all. It was all you Beth so don't give me any of this blackmail shit! You got anything else to say?"

"I love you Rob, honest to God I do and I want you back."

"People in hell want ice water Beth and they have a better chance of getting it than you have of getting me back. I'll never forget the scene of you fucking Jim in my house and on my bed and I'll never forget how easy it was for you to talk about drugging me to get me out of the way. I'm dead serious Beth. I wanted you to get a whole hell of a lot more time for what you did that a year and a day. You got anything else?"

She got up from the table and ran crying out of the bar and I got up and went home.

~~***~~

I walked into the house and the first thing Carol said to me was, "Should I start packing?"

"The only time you need to pack is for when we go on our honeymoon."

"Okay. Where are we going? How should I pack?"

She caught me flat footed with that and I stood there looking at here without speaking. "Come on Rob, speak up. Those aren't hard questions."

"Sorry, but you surprised me. When did you change your mind?"

"Last night."

"Why? What happened last night?"

"A bachelorette party that turned into an orgy. The girls that set up the party brought in a male stripper about three hours after we started drinking. He did his thing and then one of the girls hollered out, "Take it off. Take it all off" and then some of the other girls picked up the chant and so he did. He danced around with his cock swinging and Annie reached out, grabbed it and pulled it to her mouth. Marge and Gail said, "Save some for us" and Betty took off her slacks and said, "I've got to have me some of that.""

"The stripper broke free and got to his cell phone and made a call while Gail was sucking on him and twenty minutes later four guys showed up. By then Betty had fucked the stripper and Marge had sucked him hard again and had mounted him cowgirl. There was fucking going on all over the place and another three guys showed up. Bev was on her hands and knees sucking on one cock while another was fucking her from behind. I was thinking that all she was missing was one in her ass to make the picture complete and I was just the girl to show her the way.

"I had a mouth on my left tit and a cock in my hand that I was getting ready to go down on when suddenly a thought flashed through my mind. Did I really want to give up what I had in you for just some sport fucking? Just as quickly as I'd had the thought I knew the answer. I let go of the cock, pulled away from the mouth on my tit, grabbed my purse and got out of there so fast that my blouse was still open and my tits were there for all to see as I ran from the hotel room to my car.

"In a way it was stupid of me because I'd had way too much to drink to be driving, but I had to get out of there and get home where I belonged. I'm just praying that you will overlook that I did actually have a hard cock in my hand."

"It never went anywhere else?"

"No it did not."

"Okay then, I guess the question is where do you want to honeymoon?"

She smiled, grabbed my arm and started pulling me toward the bedroom.

The End

Here is a preview of another story you may also enjoy:

JUST PLAIN BOB

OPEN MIKE
NIGHT

A LANDING STRIP STORY

I came into the bar and when my eyes adjusted to the light, I looked toward the table in the back corner and saw what I expected to see. She was there with seven of her co-workers. Not counting her, there were three females and four males. She had always maintained that there was no dating going on in the group and that all they were co-workers stopping for a few drinks after work, but I knew better. I'd seen too many of them leave in pairs for me to believe that story and after seeing it too many times, I wasn't ready to believe that she wasn't doing the same thing.

I headed over and took a seat at the bar with my back to the table, but I was able to see them in the mirror behind the bar. Melody came up and set a Pabst Blue Ribbon down in front of me as she said:

"Back to do it again, I see."

"Yep."

"I'll never understand why."

"Of course, you do. Joe doesn't make me pay for my drinks and doing it keeps me off the streets and out of trouble."

"You probably already noticed that she's here."

"Yep. I saw her back there with her group."

"Why does she keep coming in?"

"Her sister says that she does it so that when I see her, I'll be reminded of what I'm missing by not going back home to her. What she apparently doesn't realize is that every time I see her with that group, I'm reminded of why I'm no longer with her."

Just then, Joe Lambert, the owner of the Landing Strip Lounge, stepped up on the platform that the bands used on Fridays and Saturdays and spoke into the microphone.

"Good evening ladies and gentlemen and welcome to open mike night at The Strip. It is good to see such a large turnout for our would be stars so without further ado, I'll turn the microphone over to our home grown master of ceremonies, Bobby Denton."

I took the stage and Joe handed me the mike. "Good evening and welcome to what I expect to be a good night here at The Strip. We have some pretty good talent here for you tonight and as always, anyone who wants to give it a try only needs to walk up and tell me and we will give you your shot.

"For those of you who are new to this, the way it works is that Joe picks a topic and our performers take Joe's topic and ad-lib their performances. Tonight's topic is President Obama's health care plan. Our performers are allowed to go off topic, but only if they have a blond joke to tell and tradition has it that I start off the show with a blond joke in honor of my wife who is blond and who detests blond jokes.

"There was this blond who married a Catholic. On their honeymoon, the blond bride slipped into a sexy nightie and, with great anticipation, crawled into bed only to find that her new Catholic husband had settled down on the couch. When she asked him why he was apparently not going to make love to her he replied:

"It's Lent."

"In tears she sobbed. 'Well that is the most ridiculous thing I've ever heard. Who did you lend it to and for how long?'"

As I finished the joke, I looked at the table where Bree was sitting and the look on her face made me smile.

"Having touched on Catholics, I'll bring up one Catholic's alternative to Obama's health care plan. A man suffered a serious heart attack while shopping in a store. The store clerks called 911 when they saw him collapse on the floor. The paramedics rushed the man to the nearest hospital where he had emergency open-heart bypass surgery.

"He awakened from the surgery to find himself in the care of the nuns at the Catholic hospital he had been taken to. A nun was seated at his bedside holding a pen and a clipboard with several forms on it. She asked him how he was going to pay for his treatment.

"Do you have insurance?" she asked.

The man relied in a raspy voice, "Ain't got no health insurance."

The nun asked, "Do you have money in the bank?"

The man replied, "Ain't got no money in the bank."

"Do you have a relative who can help you with the payments?" she asked the irritated nun.

The man said, "I only have a spinster sister and she is a nun."

The nun became agitated and loudly announced, "Nuns are not spinsters! Nuns are married to God!"

The man replied, "Perfect. Send the bill to my brother in law."

To purchase the book, look for **Open Mike Night.**

Also by this Author:

The Prodigal Family: The Abbotts

Watching My Shared Wife

The Waitress and the Runaway Husband

Baiting Mr. Little

Too Hot for Henry

Chuck's Fantasy

Wife Sharing and Other Adventures

The Redhead's Desires

Rescued at Riley's

Hazardous Wives

Wives Who Stray

His Every Fantasy

Open Mike Night

Pursuit for Revenge

From the Author

If you enjoyed any of my books then please share the love and promote my books in Amazon.

If you write me a review and send me an email I will send you a free book, or many.
(Just know that these emails are filtered by my publisher.)

Good news is always welcome.

One Last Thing, For Kindle Readers...

When you turn the page, Kindle will give you the opportunity to rate this book and share your thoughts on Facebook and Twitter. If you enjoyed my writings, would you please take a few seconds to let your friends know about it? Because... when they enjoy they will be grateful to you and so will I.

Thank You!

An Open Letter from Just Plain Bob

A message for those who like my stories, those who hate my stories, those who are indifferent and those who have yet to make up their minds.

I have often stated that I really don't care what others think about my stories, that I write for my own enjoyment and then I offer to share. If you like my stories fine and if you don't, also fine since I have already satisfied my target audience - me!

It is human nature to strive to get better. If you take up bowling your first games are going low scoring, but you will work and practice to get better and as your average climbs you may forget the game where you had three gutter balls and shot an eighty-six, but that game is still there in your past.

Your first time on the golf course you shot an eighty on the front nine, but did you settle for that being your game or did you work to improve? You may eventually get a three handicap, but that nine hole eighty is still there as part of your past.

When you hired in at your job did you say, "Cool, I got it made" and do nothing more than what you barely had to do or did you go to work thinking that, "Someday I'm going to be running this place." You might never climb that high, but human nature says that you are going to at least try.

It is the same with authors who write stories and post them on sites like Literotica. Their first stories might not be all that good, but comments and feedback along with a desire to get better drive them toward putting out a better product or to at least try.

I'm no different. My first stories might not have been all that great, but they are still there on the hard drive. I like cheating wife stories and five years ago I found my first adult site that catered to cheating wife stories. It was a pay site, but it had a policy of giving a free lifetime membership to anyone who submitted five stories to the site. How hard can that be I said to myself as I sat down and fired up the word processor and went to work.

I sent my five stories in and sat back to enjoy my free membership and a funny thing happened. I started getting feedback, most of it positive, and I became hooked. I started cranking out more stories. The site I was sending my stories to had seven categories:

Bisexual
Cream Pie

Groups
I Watch
Gang Bang
Racial
SM/BD

I know nothing about bisexual or SM/BD and I had no interest in Groups so all the stories I wrote I tailored for the four remaining categories:

Cream Pie
I Watch
Gang Bang
Racial.

I turned out eight stories a month, two for each category, which means that after five years I have over 120 stories in each of those categories and they are all still on the hard drive.

A year ago I received an email asking me why I never posted stories on Literotica. The answer? I didn't know about Lit. I pulled it up, liked what I saw, and started sending in stories to it. All new stories? No, not hardly, not with over 400 stories sitting on the hard drive. Maybe one new story for each fifteen or so old ones. The newer ones are better, at least I think they are and I have received some feedback that leads me to believe that others think so too, and I will continue to write new ones.

But I am still going to recycle what is on the hard drive, stories that were written specifically to fit the four categories. That means that those of you who hate cream pie stories still have eighty or so to look forward to. Ditto for those who call me a racist; you will get another seventy or so interracial stories.

Those who hate wimps will only see about fifty more of those because the stories I sent to the I Watch category were split 50/50 between what some call wimps and some call "real men." Why the 50/50 split? It came from listening to the readers. I would get feedback asking me why all the men in my stories were hard asses. "In real life men are more forgiving, especially if it is the first indiscretion." So I would write stories with forgiving husbands and boyfriends and then the next batch of feedback would say, "Why are all your husbands spineless wimps" and I'd write stories that went back the other way.

Eventually I came to realize that I was wasting my time - there was no way I could write a story that would satisfy everybody and that is when I adopted my philosophy of writing for my own enjoyment and then offering to share.

As far as the gangbang stories? Well, what can I say? Gangbangs are gangbangs and there are still eighty or so of them to go.

The bottom line is that Literotica readers are going to see more of my old stories than my new ones. If I'm still around three or four years from now it will probably go the other way, more new than old.

I feel the need to respond to some of the comments and emails I have received. By far the largest percentage comes from people who say, "You are an asshole because all women are not whores and sluts and that's all you make them out to be."

Next most common is, "You must really hate women you sick fuck."

"You must be a wimp because all the men in your stories are wimps" is up there in the top ten along with, "Why don't you give it a rest and go crawl off in a hole somewhere."

There is a lot more, but I'm only going to address those four and in reverse order.

I won't stop and go crawl in a hole because I am enjoying the hell out of what I am doing and remember what I said, I am doing this for MY OWN ENJOYMENT and then I offer to share. Some obviously like my sharing with them and so I will continue to do so. No one is holding a gun to a reader's head and telling them they must click on a Just Plain Bob story or die. It is a conscious choice on the reader's part to move that mouse and click on that story.

When a man finds out he has a cheating wife or girlfriend there are only a limited number of ways he can handle it. If he loves her he can forgive, try to forget and try to hold on and somehow make things work. He can turn his back on her, walk away and get on with his life. The third option is to take revenge.

According to a good portion of those who send me feedback the first and second options are proof that the men are wimps. If the man takes the third option he is still considered a wimp if he doesn't do some sort of physical damage to the woman and her lover. These readers believe that the only way not to be a wimp is to kill, maim and destroy everything in sight. Doing that however, will invariably get the man throw in jail and that is why it so rarely happens in real life.

In real life most revenge takes place in the man's head when he says to himself, "I should have _____ (fill in the blank) the fucking cunt!" I know this because I have been there and done that (see The Dark Trilogy). In my stories I try to mirror real life so kill, maim and destroy are going to be for the most part absent. Outside of some fisticuffs there will be very little physical violence in my stories. Most of my husbands are going to do what I did, what several of my friends and others that I know have done, forgive, or walk away. If this makes them wimps and me a wimp for writing the story that way, so be it.

Next is the "I must hate all women." Nothing could be farther from the truth. I love women. I lust after women. I even like whores and sluts. I have been married four times, engaged two other times (that did not end in marriage) and I have always had girlfriends between marriages. My philosophy is that women were put on this earth for me to enjoy and I'm not talking just sexually. I could sit at the mall (and have) for hours and just girl watch.

The engagements, girlfriends and three of the four marriages bring me to the #1 anti JPB comment on the list.

"You are an asshole because all women aren't whores and sluts."

Well dear reader, you can not prove that by me! I will say up front that I KNOW all women aren't whores and sluts, BUT the majority of the women in my life were. My mother ran around on my father for years while he was driving a truck for a living. My Aunt Margaret cheated regularly on my Uncle Bill, as did my Aunt Mildred on my Uncle Paul. My Aunt Betty fucked around on my Uncle Bob for years and finally left him for his brother, my Uncle Wendell. Uncle Wendell in turn caught her on her knees at his company Christmas party giving Season's Greetings to his boss.

My sister is three times divorced and each divorce came about when the then current husband caught her out spreading pollen. Both of the engagements I mentioned ended when I found out that I was not the one and only and a lot of the girls I dated between marriages never made it to engagement status for the same reason.

And that brings me to my three ex-wives. The first one, Helen (I believe I commented on her in the intro to The Dark Trilogy) had seven different lovers before I found out what was going on. I was living proof that love is blind. Ditto with my second wife. She had a secret life that she hid from me and when I found out about her brother, his friends and the gangbangs she was history.

My third marriage ended in divorce because of a different kind of cheating (and I can just imagine the outrage I am going to get over this) - she cheated on me with an idea. I was away from home on business, she was lonely, a couple of Jehovah's Witnesses knocked on the door and my wife, with nothing better to do invited them in. When I came home from my trip I found out that she had found God. On a scale that runs from TRUE BELIEVER on one end to ATHEIST on the other you will find me just to the right of AGNOSTIC and since I would not allow myself to be SAVED the marriage eventually died.

So yes, I write about sluts and whores because as everyone knows, you tend to write about the things you know. And I do like sluts and whores, just not the ones that lie to me and cheat on me.

So be forewarned - if you click on a Just Plain Bob story you will be getting sluts, whores and husbands who do not kill, maim and destroy. There are other things you will rarely find in a Just Plain Bob story. Even though I try to mirror real life my stories all take place in StoryLand. In StoryLand STDs and un-wanted pregnancies do not exist unless the author feels like they may add something to the story. Bad things do not happen in StoryLand unless the author so wills it and no amount of "You should have…" in comments and feedback will change a story already posted.

Lastly, I will touch on a truth. None of what I have written here means shit because the same readers will still read the same stories that they profess to hate and make the same comments they have always made. Knowing this, I will deliberately post stories that will have them frothing at the mouth.

It is the least I can do for an adoring public.

Thank you!

Just Plain Bob
justplainbob@awesomeauthors.org